# NOT GUILTY!

# Not Guilty!
## To Forgive is Divine

Noel Stewart

*AuthorHouse™*
*1663 Liberty Drive*
*Bloomington, IN 47403*
*www.authorhouse.com*
*Phone: 1-800-839-8640*


*© 2013 by Noel Stewart. All rights reserved.*

*No part of this book may be reproduced, stored in a retrieval system, or transmitted by any means without the written permission of the author.*

*Published by AuthorHouse   06/17/2013*

*ISBN: 978-1-4817-6670-8 (sc)*
*ISBN: 978-1-4817-6671-5 (e)*

*Library of Congress Control Number: 2013911028*


*Any people depicted in stock imagery provided by Thinkstock are models, and such images are being used for illustrative purposes only.*
*Certain stock imagery © Thinkstock.*

*This book is printed on acid-free paper.*

*Because of the dynamic nature of the Internet, any web addresses or links contained in this book may have changed since publication and may no longer be valid. The views expressed in this work are solely those of the author and do not necessarily reflect the views of the publisher, and the publisher hereby disclaims any responsibility for them.*

To my beloved wife, Annalisa.

And in loving memory of my parents, Hamilton and Joan Stewart.

*Therefore let him who thinks he stands
take heed lest he fall.*
*1 Corinthians 10:12 (NKJV)*

The Arima Magistrates Court in the small Caribbean island of Trinidad was not a majestic building with fantastic mahogany doors and intricate designs that would hold someone's attention in stupendous awe nor would they find themselves lost in oblivion. No, it was just another rundown, unkempt, almost a shack of a building surrounded by rum shops, haberdasheries, government offices and myriads of people traversing or liming along the streets. This was an everyday occurrence except on Sundays, where the streets became a ghost town and all businesses as well as offices were closed.

Some people milled around to see the prisoners being brought out in handcuffs from trucks that looked like armored cages, while others saw it as an inconvenience where heavily armed police officers would block the road to prevent traffic, human or otherwise from venturing near their path. The prisoners were then hustled through the back entrance like a herd of cattle, some pleading their innocence, others crying for their mothers while hiding their faces. But for the crowd which would have gathered by now, there was always one prisoner who was the show stopper. He would receive the brunt of the jeers and stares from the unforgiving public usually for a crime that made headlines in the daily newspapers.

"Wicked beast! Hang him! Jail him for life!" were some of the words that were sometimes heard being shouted about by the agitated crowd. It was a bit ironic though, how the worst inmates were able to hire the best lawyers to defend them. However, there was one particular female lawyer who was also among the best. She stood for what was right and honest. Some saw her as being perfect, a little too perfect.

In this town everybody's guilty until they were proven innocent, but even if they were proven innocent they were still guilty according to street justice and street justice would only be satisfied by the sweet taste of revenge. Some believed that the judicial system was responsible for the numerous amounts of criminals in society because of the lengthy time it took for a court matter to be heard. Sometimes, it is easier to take matters into your own hands and let the defendant experience what you have been through. At least, so it seemed. Justice delayed is justice denied as the saying goes. Life for some can really be cold sometimes.

*Yet if anyone suffers as a Christian, let him not be ashamed, but let him glorify God in this matter.*
*1 Peter 4:16 (NKJV)*

Such coldness was usually experienced in the courtrooms where the silent screams of justice and revenge could be heard along the corridors of the aged old building. Guilty! Guilty! Guilty! The sound would echo over and over again. However, in some cases it was easier to prove someone innocent of a crime that he committed than to prove that he was guilty of the same crime. The burden of proof lies with the arguments put forward before the court.

This particular court room was no different. Standing there late one afternoon was a female attorney packing her briefcase, getting ready to leave after winning a child custody matter. That was her field and she was good at it, very good. Slim shaped, well dressed with perfectly manicured finger nails, high heels and designer eyewear. Her attractiveness was further accentuated by the way she carried herself—direct and to the point, a woman in complete control. She could argue a case to the very end, stand toe to toe against any counsel on the other side of the bench and change the very mood of the jury to the one that suits her with her compelling closing statements. Her female colleagues envied her and her male counterparts felt threatened by her because she had such a domineering, alpha provocative attitude. She was metro bad.

> *For the time has come for judgment to begin at the house of God; and if it begins with us first, what will be the end of those who do not obey the gospel of God?*
> *1 Peter 4:17 (NKJV)*

"This place needs a good paint job." It was the voice of a man who was also well dressed. Rhonda did not know when he entered the room or just how long he was standing there. He was tall, light skinned and clean shaven. He wore a black tailored suit that matched the color of his eyes - black. His shiny shoes were pointed at the tip and they appeared to be made out of snake skin. He was someone who looked impressive and intimidating at the same time. "Man has become so creative in the things they do. What was once thought to be impossible is now a reality. If the mind can think it, it can be achieved. Yes?" He waited for an answer but there was none.

The female attorney barely even looked at the man. In fact, she just shrugged her shoulder and continued what she was doing before.

The man was a little more direct this time. "I saw the way you handled that child custody case. I must say I'm impressed. You made the child's father look so incompetent. The way I see it, why have any children when you cannot take care of them in the first place? I just don't get it. Understand what I'm saying?"

At this point the female attorney was ready to leave. "No!" and with that she headed for the door. The man walked behind her with both hands in his pant pockets. "No? Can I ask you a question before you leave?" The female attorney turned around and for the first time they were staring each other face to face. The man's eyes were cold, dark and probing. His face was expressionless almost trance-like. He showed no emotions. The female attorney felt the discomfort but did not show it. Being the professional she was, she held her ground. "Go ahead" she said.

"Do you know who Jane Doe is?" the man asked without blinking or using any gestures—just staring, probing. What was he looking for? There was a subtle, lingering, hissing sound in his voice that was more pronounced when he said certain words. Rhonda could not help but notice.

"Jane Doe is not a real name" she said. "It is used when some female is unidentified. For someone as well dressed as you and smart looking, it's expected that you should know that. Or maybe you are interested in something that is way above your league?" Rhonda then turned and walked away. The man was not ready to give up so easily. And so for a very brief moment he went into the defensive mode. "You know what, you are right. I do have another interest". He smiled wryly and waited for the perfect time. The female attorney was still walking away but that did not stop the man from talking. "I do believe you know who Jane Doe is or . . . was. She would have been six years old today." What he said stopped the female attorney in her tracks.

> *Be sober, be vigilant; because your adversary the devil walks about like a roaring lion, seeking whom he may devour.*
> *1 Peter 5:8 (NKJV)*

The words cut into her like a glowing red hot soldering blade. The tone of the man's voice changed into a deep eerie sound as though something ominous was going to happen. Was it his tone or the revelation of the deep dark secret that started the turmoil and nightmare in the head of the female attorney? She was showing weakness. Silence . . . . no response. The man came closer. His steps echoing as he approached her down the corridor; closer and closer until he was just a whisper away. He walked with a swagger each step measured. He too was a professional at what he did and now he was about to build his case.

"Has success clouded your mind Rhonda?" Hmmm ... he knows my name. He knows me. Maybe somebody told him about me. But I don't know him. Is he an attorney also? Maybe he attended law school with me. I have never seen him before. But only my friends called me by my first name. Horror and confusion flooded the mind of Rhonda Smith as memories of her past came flashing before her. She tried in vain to figure out who this man was and what he wanted.

Born in a depressed neighborhood, Rhonda had determined to make something worthwhile of her life. She had one younger sister and two older brothers and they all looked out for each other. Although her mother was a housewife she did domestic work wherever and whenever the opportunity arose. Her father was a skilled handyman who could do any kind of menial labor. Fortunately he was hardly ever out of a job.

> *Resist him, steadfast in the faith, knowing that the same sufferings are experienced by your brotherhood in the world.*
> *1 Peter 5:9 (NKJV)*

The man continued drilling, immediately snapping Rhonda out of her daydream. "Six years ago a young girl walked into a medical clinic after finding out that she was pregnant. She paid a thousand dollars cash to the doctor who performed the routine procedure and . . . . Jane Doe was no more. "You know" pausing for effect, "if Jane Doe had lived I'm sure she would have been a nice, pretty little girl just like her mommy."

The swipe the man took at Rhonda was deep—deep enough to cause her to drop her head and gaze into nothingness. If only the earth could open up and swallow her she would have jumped at the opportunity in order to escape the memories.

The man made sure that such an opportunity would never come and so he continued unrelentingly. "Oooooh, I think I struck a nerve. So you do remember." Rhonda had to prop herself up against a wall because her legs were now failing her. She refused to look at her aggressor. Was it shame or guilt? She could not defend herself. She needed time for a rebuttal. Too late. Time's up. The man's method of delivering his onslaught now turned into sinister sarcasm. "So . . . . Rhonda, tell me something. What were you thinking when you went into that clinic. Did you believe that the memories would just disappear into thin air? Did you believe that no one would have known your secret? That life would continue to be normal? Wrong!! After what you did, your life could never be normal. Remember, somebody is always watching. You cannot hide. Not even your deepest darkest secrets." Rhonda's knees began to buckle. She wanted to run but something was preventing her, blocking her path, pulling her back and pressing her down. There was a whirlwind of woes going on in her head. Forces, unseen forces penetrating her mind capsizing neatly folded logical thoughts that took years to put away. They were all being pulled down and tossed everywhere. What were they looking for? She had to sit down.

"Rhonda!" The sound of her name immediately snapped her back into reality. The man was not finished. "What you did was not all that bad. Women all over the world are having abortions every day. There are advocates for these things, the feminists, the humanists, family planning, you made a choice and that's ok. You went in the medical facility and you came out . . . . alive! The abortion was safe and it was your right to choose." Tears were welling up in Rhonda's eyes as she sat on the floor looking down the corridor that seemed so never ending.

*For we do not wrestle against flesh and blood, but against principalities, against powers, against the rulers of the darkness of this age, against spiritual hosts of wickedness in the heavenly places.*
*Ephesians 6:12 (NKJV)*

The man was standing over her now looking at her with disdain, shaking his head at the pitiful sight. "Why are you so sad Rhonda? Okay, I see. You joined a church." His tone changed into one of hopelessness. "What are you looking for, acceptance? Please . . . you are a successful lawyer, what are you doing around those people? You know, if they were to find out about your personal life could you imagine the amount of hell, I mean, what a hard time, those same church people would give you?"

Whether it was fear or courage Rhonda finally said something but not before she coughed, a simple cough which she has had for years but had grown accustomed to. "Why are you bringing up my past?" She finally caught her breath. "That is none of your business. I thought I dealt with that already?"

"OBJECTION!!!!!" The bolstering retort from the man was enough to make Rhonda cringe and to seek refuge against an unforgiving cold and callous wall. "You thought? The defendant is giving an opinion. For someone as well dressed as you and smart looking, you should know that. Opinions are not evidence." He was mocking her and there was a smirk on his face. She was almost certain that she saw what appeared to be fangs. But in a state of disorientation, who knows? The man began pacing the floor like a predator about to devour his prey.

"Church is an emotional place that gives people a false sense of hope that one day they would all live forever in a world where there would be no sickness or pain, guilt or sorrow. Amen and amen! It is nothing but a house for hypocrites and gossip! How could you expect to change the lives of others when yours is in a mess?"

Rhonda was trying to find strength. "What do you want?" she asked, her voice cracking with the very words she spoke. Sensing victory, a broad smile appeared on the man's face and suddenly he bursts into laughter. "This is too easy!" he quipped. "Where is the fight? Have you no backbone? Unbelievable!! No closing arguments? This is absolutely amazing. Tell you what, since you have made it so easy this is what I want." He paused in theatrical character. "I want . . . . your soul."

*Therefore take up the whole armor of God, that you may be able to withstand in the evil day, and having done all, to stand.*
*Ephesians 6:13 (NKJV)*

"My what?" Rhonda could not believe what she was hearing. The cold hand of fear overtook her.

"You heard what I said" the man shouted. "Why are you acting so surprised? Six years ago you took a life. That sets a precedent, and a precedent becomes law and I am here to ensure that that law is carried out."

"Mister, you must be crazy. Who are you?"

The man stopped pacing the floor, looked up at the ceiling and introduced himself. "My friends call me Mentor but you can call me Tom." He paused for effect as a cold chill entered the room. Rhonda felt it, but could not tell from where it came because all the windows were closed. She tried standing up but she could not find the strength. "Oh God" she gasped and coughed again. "Help me Jesus!"

Mentor had heard enough. "Help you? How many families have you destroyed in this courtroom Rhonda? And why? Is it because you don't have a family to call your own? Or is it because of this emotional scar that you have that you now hate all men? Well, I have a question for you Rhonda, so listen and listen well. Who . . . was the father of the child?"

Screams. Tears. Her face was in a mess and her hair all disheveled like that of a wet furry wild animal. "Mercy Jesus!!" she cried and wept bitterly.

It was the cry of a weeping mother who lost her only child because of a mistake she made. Life for her had never been the same. Behind the façade and the professional success she achieved, this particular chapter of her life was never closed. No matter how hard she tried to get over it, something always reminded her of this one weakness that made her vulnerable. So, she was not perfect after all.

*For the weapons of our warfare are not carnal but mighty in God for pulling down strongholds,*
*2 Corinthians 10:4 (NKJV)*

"Was it Frank, Samuel, Derek or maybe it was John Doe?" Mentor pressed on. Memories of her past came flashing before her again like a raging tumultuous twister. The many broken relationships she had in the past were so devastating that true love was never found. Abused and misused, lied upon and mistreated by men; all kinds of men. All Rhonda wanted was to be loved and to feel wanted; to be held and cuddled just as her father did to her mom; to have a family that was as close as the one she grew up with but not an unplanned one. Who was the father? That was anyone's guess.

Mentor continued mercilessly. "Look what I have found." Mentor reached into his pocket and took out a baby rattle. "Remember this Rhonda? Your great grandmother handed this down to your mother, and your mother handed it down to you, and you handed it down to . . . NO ONE!!!!" Mentor throws the rattle to the ground towards Rhonda. His voice echoed through the corridor like rolling thunder. "Rhonda, the torment can stop you know, just come to me." He stretched his right hand towards her, motioning her to come. "Tell you what, let's make a deal. You work for me and we'll force this government to implement laws, not just any kind of law but pro abortion laws. That way, I will not tell on you. I will not tell your friends or your enemies. This Warriors for Jesus group, the one that you are president of would not know a thing."

Rhonda, although weak physically, still had the strength or was it courage to say no but not before she coughed. "You know" said Mentor, "you should really check a doctor about that nagging cough. The common cold is a terrible virus." Mentor draws closer to Rhonda's ears and whispered "but then again so is HIV." And with that there were peals of laughter as though he had won a resounding victory. His eyes narrowed towards Rhonda as he spoke. "You can't play with the dog and don't expect to be bitten by the fleas and oh how they are biting now!!! That was the chance you took; and just in case you do not know, the child's father has already died. Let me give you some time to reminisce, but then again you don't have much time either." Mentor then turned and walked away quite abhorrently, laughing his way into a distant room.

*Casting down arguments and every high thing that exalts itself against the knowledge of God, bringing every thought into captivity to the obedience of Christ;*
*2 Corinthians 10:5 (NKJV)*

By this time Rhonda was completely beside herself, like a helpless, hapless, discarded raggedy doll, torn apart and tossed aside. The tears were overflowing and uncontrollable. Suicide appeared beside her with his arms outstretched and guilt was ever present cajoling her. DO IT!! DO IT!! HOW LONG MUST THIS GO ON FOR!! IT'S TOO MUCH SHAME!!

If there was ever a time that Rhonda needed to prove that God existed it was now. Although the words were not forming in her mouth, there was something being said from the heart. Somehow she remembered songs she sang as a child in church Sunday School. Songs like Jesus Be a Fence; He's My Rock, My Sword and My Shield and Jesus Loves the Little Children. But she just did not have the strength to sing. There was no joy or peace of mind that the preacher talked about. Oh where was that mustard seed faith that would move mountains Jesus? . . . . Jesus!!? Jesus!!? There was something about that name. She was saying it over and over in her mind. It gave a flicker of hope, a ray of light that was bright enough to reveal the evidence of things not seen. Say the Name. Speak the Name, BELIEVE THE NAME.

Rhonda was trembling. "Jesus." A whisper came out from her mouth. "Jesus, Jesus" . . . her courage was building. "JESUS!!! JESUS!!!! HELP ME JESUS!!!! IT'S ME JESUS, HELP ME PLEASE . . . . JESUS!!!!" The cries were loud and desperate but sincere. Suicide fled and guilt saw a reflection of himself. It was pitiful. He ran like a bat out of hell. Rhonda's arms were raised towards the heavens without a care. She felt strength and before long she was on her knees. Joy got a hold of her and finally, there was a smile on her face. Peace was her comfort and she remained still just long enough to hear the voice of a man coming towards her down the corridor. He spoke as though he was giving the opening argument of a case in a courtroom. And although the voice was quite authoritative, he was very convincing and direct. He meant business and was dressed for it. Today was the day for wearing tailor made suits and shiny shoes.

> *Therefore submit to God. Resist the devil and he will flee from you.*
> *James 4:7 (NKJV)*

"Therefore, if anyone be in Christ, that person is a new creation; old things are passed away and behold all things are become new." He looked tenderly towards her "On your feet Rhonda, do not be afraid. You have overcome because greater is He that is in you than he that is in the world."

"Not so fast! Not . . . so . . . fast!" It was Mentor. He had positioned himself for a challenge or a duel to the end, if necessary. "The soul that sins shall surely die" he said ominously with impending doom. This was a different kind of law from the one that Rhonda practiced in the courtroom.

"If anyone confesses his sins He is faithful and just to forgive him and cleanse him of all unrighteousness." It was a quick rebuttal by the stranger.

Wait! Those words were from the Bible. Rhonda suddenly realized that her very existence, the foundation of her belief, whether she deserved to live or die was being debated right before her eyes and the Bible was both witness and evidence for and against her. What she believed or did not believe determined her destiny.

"The wages of sin is death!" Mentor spoke with poisonous venom; his voice was growing with impatience and his eyes and eyebrows narrowed into one. Rhonda saw what appeared to be a snake. Although Mentor wore a suit, his true character was unfolding, shedding.

"Rhonda, don't be afraid. God has given you a gift and His gift is eternal life. That is what you have and that is what no one can take away." Those words the stranger spoke were soft, gentle and reassuring. It actually brought comfort and cheer to Rhonda. She could not remember the last time she experienced such a feeling. It felt like an eternity.

"To be carnally minded is death!" Mentor growled.

"But, to be spiritually minded is life and peace." The stranger looked at Rhonda with those loving eyes and continued speaking, this time rhetorically. Rhonda, did you know that there are some who go about wandering the streets like vagrants without a fixed place of abode, trying to make other people's lives miserable just like theirs? Do you know anybody like that Rhonda? Hmm . . . uhhh . . . hmm?" The stranger raised his eyebrows and made quick glances at Mentor; his eyes going to and fro, his head twitching in unison. Rhonda mimicked the actions of the stranger and replied with sarcasm. "Oh nooo!! Of course not! Do you? Hmmm . . . . uhhh . . . hmm?" She was beginning to enjoy this and the mere presence of the stranger reassured her.

Mentor felt as though he was being mocked. He became annoyed and started shouting. "Know this. The unrighteous shall not enter into the Kingdom. Nor fornicators, idolaters, homosexuals, thieves, revelers, liars, MURDERERS!!!" pointing at Rhonda. Mentor felt he had won and pulled out a long chain with shackles to take Rhonda away.

There was a moment of silence before the stranger spoke. He stared deeply into Mentor's eyes and saw fear and hopelessness looking back at him. "And some of those things she was" he said gently. "But now," turning towards Rhonda, "she has been washed, sanctified, justified in the name of Jesus and by the Spirit of the Lord."

"INNOCENT BLOOD WAS SHED!!" Mentor shouted.

The stranger was calm and again stared directly into Mentor's eyes. "Say it again."

"INNOCENT BLOOD WAS SHED!!"

"Say it again."

"INNOCENT BLO" . . . he snarled. Suddenly realizing what he was saying all along Mentor covered his mouth in shock and horror.

It was time to put this case under wraps and that was what the stranger did. His voice rose as he spoke with authority. "There is therefore now no condemnation to them who are in Christ Jesus, who walk not after the flesh but after the Spirit." The tables had turned. Mentor was cringing. Now he was in torment. The stranger's words nullified every argument that rendered Mentor speechless. The stranger paced the floor with grace and mastery; he was in an attacking mode. "Who shall lay any charge against God's

*Not Guilty!*

elect? You!? It is God who justifies. Who is he who condemns? How dare you!! How dare . . . YOU!! You have no right! It is Christ who died and rose again. He makes intercession for his children because He loves them including her." The stranger looked at Rhonda and declared with a thunderous voice "IF THE SON THEREFORE SHALL MAKE YOU FREE, YOU . . . SHALL BE FREE INDEED." The stranger slapped a nearby desk in the corridor and shouted "NOT GUILTY!!"

Mentor made one last stance and charged towards Rhonda. "Arrrgh!!! Oaf!" Mentor did not know what hit him. All he knew was that he was on the floor writhing in pain with a stranger standing over him with a sword drawn. The stranger's eyes were fixed and his voice deep with conviction. "You have two choices; you either leave in peace or . . . . in pieces. Case closed!" Mentor chose the former and disappeared into oblivion whimpering in pain and embarrassment.

Rhonda finally spoke. "Who, how, I, I, don't . . . ." She was lost for words and so the stranger helped her find them. "Rhonda, say the Name. Believe in His Name. Call upon His Name." And with that, the stranger was gone.

THE END

Edwards Brothers Malloy
Oxnard, CA USA
November 11, 2013